The New Adventures of
Curious George

Library of Congress Catalog Card Number: 99-73442
ISBN-13: 978-0-618-66373-6
ISBN-10: 0-618-66373-8
Manufactured in the United States of America
DOW 10 9 8 7 6 5 4 3 2

The New Adventures of Curious George

Margret *and* H. A. Rey

Illustrated in the style of H. A. Rey by Vipah Interactive

Houghton Mifflin Company
Boston 2006

The New Adventures of
Curious George

Contents

MARGRET & H.A. REY'S

Curious George

Goes to a Chocolate Factory

Illustrated in the style of H. A. Rey by Vipah Interactive

Houghton Mifflin Company   Boston

This is George.

George was a good little monkey and always very curious.

One day George went for a drive with his friend, the man with the yellow hat.

"Look, George," the man said. "There's a store in that chocolate factory up ahead. Let's stop for a treat."

George loved chocolates. Inside the store, boxes of chocolates were stacked everywhere, but the man with the yellow hat found his favorites right away. "George," he said, "wait here while I buy these, and please stay out of trouble."

George looked around the store.
He saw chocolate-covered cherries
and fudge-flavored lollipops.
A chocolate bunny caught his eye.

Then something else caught his eye.
What were all those people looking at?
George was curious.

He climbed up to get a better look. Through the window he saw lots of trays filled with little brown dots.

What were all those little brown dots?

George was curious.
He found a door that led
to the other side of the window.

The little brown dots were chocolates, of course! A tour guide was showing a group of people how to tell what was inside the chocolates by looking at the swirls on top.

This little swirl
means fudge,

this one says that
caramel is inside,

and this wiggle is for
marshmallow.

This is the squiggle
for a truffle,

this one is
for nougat,

this sideways swirl is
for orange fluff,

and this one is for George's favorite — banana cream.

George followed the tour group until they came to a balcony overlooking a room where the chocolates were made. Down below, busy workers picked the candy off the machines and put them in boxes.

These were the machines that made the chocolates with the swirls on top! The chocolates came out of the machines on long belts. But how did they get their swirls?

George was curious.

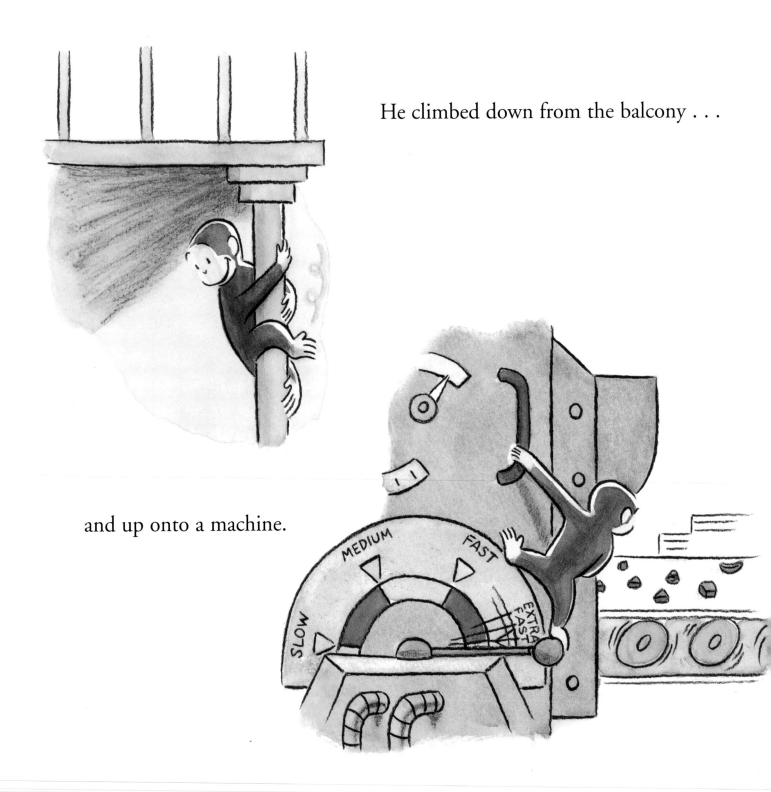

He climbed down from the balcony . . .

and up onto a machine.

George peeked inside.
He was trying to see what
was making the swirls when
all of a sudden . . .

the chocolates began
coming out faster and
faster! They sped by him
so quickly they seemed
to be running on legs
of their own.

"Quick! Bring more boxes!" yelled a man with a tall white hat.
"What happened?" asked another man.

Nobody answered. Nobody knew what had happened and everyone was so busy that no one noticed George.

The workers began to fall behind and the candy began to fall off the end of the belt.

"Save the chocolates!" yelled the man with the tall white hat.

Meanwhile, George saw one of his favorites whiz by. He tried to catch the banana-cream chocolate, but it was too fast!

He chased it to the end of the belt.

At the end of the belt a pile of chocolates was growing taller and taller. George had never seen so many chocolates!

As he searched for the banana cream, he put the others in empty boxes.

George was a fast worker. Someone noticed and yelled, "Bring that monkey more boxes! He's helping us catch up!"

Not all the chocolates made it into boxes, but no more chocolates fell on the floor.

Just when George and the workers were all caught up, the tour guide ran in with the man with the yellow hat. "Get that monkey out of here!" she yelled. "He's ruining our chocolates!"

"But this little monkey SAVED the chocolates," explained the workers.

Then the man with the tall white hat said to George, "You may have caused us some trouble, but you were a speedy little monkey. You deserve a big box of candy for all your help."

George was glad he was not in trouble, but he did not take the chocolates.

Back in the parking lot, the workers waved good-bye as George and his friend got into their little blue car.

"George, are you sure you don't want any chocolates before we leave?" asked the man with the yellow hat.

George was sure.

MARGRET & H.A.REY'S

Curious George

and the Puppies

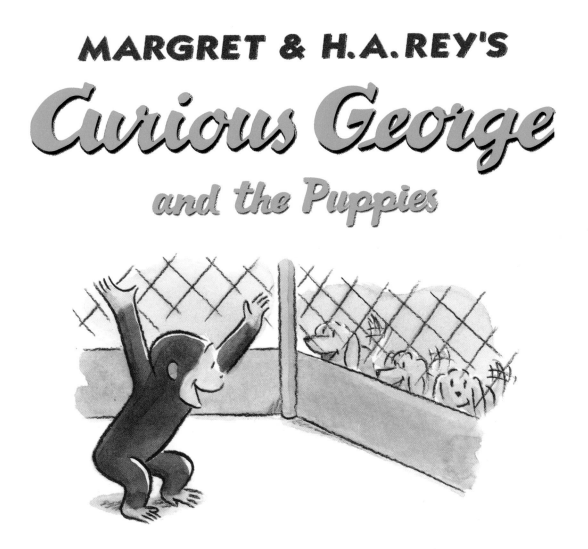

Illustrated in the style of H. A. Rey by Vipah Interactive

Houghton Mifflin Company   Boston

This is George.

George was a good little monkey and always very curious.

One day George went for a walk with his friend, the man with the yellow hat.

When they sat down to rest, they noticed a tiny kitten peeking out from under a bush. The kitten looked frightened.

"Perhaps she is lost," said the man with the yellow hat.

Together, he and George searched the park for the little kitten's owner.

But the kitten was all alone.

"This kitten is too young to be on her own," the man said. "We should take her to the animal shelter, where they can care for her and find her a home."

So George and the kitten and the man with the yellow hat drove to the animal shelter.

The director of the shelter was glad to see them. "It was good of you to bring the kitten here," she said. "We will be happy to take care of her."

George gave the kitten to the director, then he and the man with the yellow hat walked inside.

"Come in," the director said, "but watch where you step. We have a large litter of puppies and one has gotten out of his cage. We're still looking for him, so please be careful."

She closed the door quickly behind them.

George had never been to an animal shelter before. Animals of all kinds were being cared for here. George saw bunnies, cats, turtles, and guinea pigs. He even saw a snake.

But he didn't see any puppies.

"George, I need to sign some papers," said the man with
the yellow hat. "Please stay here and don't be too curious."

Just as the man with the yellow hat
left the room, George heard barking.
Maybe it was the puppies!
   But where was it coming from?
   George was curious.

He followed the
barking noises . . .

and found a room full of dogs! There were yellow dogs, spotted dogs, sleek dogs, and fluffy dogs. There were quiet dogs and yappy dogs and even a dog without a tail. But where were the puppies?

Then George saw a
little wagging tail.

Then another.

And another!

Once George saw the puppies, he could not take his eyes off them.

He had to pet one.

Here was a puppy!
The puppy liked George.

George wanted to hold the puppy. Slowly, he opened the door . . .

but before George could even reach the puppy, the mother dog
pushed the door open and was off like a shot! George tried to close
the door after her, but the puppies were too fast!

There was nothing George could do.

Puppies were everywhere!

Puppies hid under the desk. Puppies barked at bunnies.
One puppy played with a telephone cord and another climbed
on top of a cage to watch the others get into mischief.

Soon all the dogs were barking, the cats were meowing,
and the bunnies rustled into the corner of their cage.

"Oh no!" cried the director as she and the man with the yellow hat rushed into the room. "Now ALL the puppies are out!"

The man with the yellow hat helped the director gather up the puppies and put them safely back in their cage. Soon all the animals settled down and were quiet.

Except for one.
Who was still barking?
It was the mother dog!
What was she barking at? There was nothing here but a door.

There must be something on the other side, thought George.

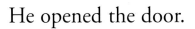
He opened the door.

45

It was the missing puppy! Everyone was happy to finally find the
puppy. The director scooped him up and said, "George, you certainly
caused a ruckus! But if you hadn't let the puppies out, we might still
be searching for this little one."

Then she gave the puppies and their mother a snack.

"These puppies are now big enough to go live with families who will take care of them," she said. "Do you want to take one home with you, George?"

George did.

MARGRET & H.A. REY'S
Curious George
Makes Pancakes

Illustrated in the style of H. A. Rey by Vipah Interactive

Houghton Mifflin Company   Boston

This is George.

George was a good little monkey and always very curious.

One morning the man with the yellow hat woke George early.

"Time to get up, George," he said. "The pancake breakfast is today."

George loved the pancake breakfast. It was a fundraiser held every
year to make money for special programs at the children's hospital.

Besides eating pancakes, there were all kinds of games to play. Even the mayor came to play and eat, but first he gave a welcome speech.

"Thank you all for coming," the mayor said. "We appreciate your generous support."

He thanked all the volunteers who were helping that day and finally he said, "Please enjoy yourselves...

and the pancakes!"

When the mayor finished, the man with the yellow hat said, "George, I'm going to buy our tickets. Please wait here and don't be too curious."

George waited like a good little monkey, but — *mmm!* — something smelled good!

Could it be the pancakes?
George was curious.

He followed the delicious smell and found a whole griddle full of pancakes! George watched as a man poured little batter circles and flipped them up in the air.

It looked like fun to make pancakes!

George wanted to help.

On a table near the griddle was a basket full of blueberries.

These pancakes need blueberries, George thought. And he sprinkled some on top.

Meanwhile, the man
at the griddle was so busy
he didn't notice the little monkey
helping him. But the line grew and grew...

George's pancakes were a hit! Soon everyone wanted them and the man could not keep up. "Please wait," he said to someone holding an empty plate. "I need to find an assistant to help me." And just like that, he was gone.

George looked at the people waiting in line and then at the empty griddle. Why, he could make pancakes. He could be the assistant!

George poured the batter into
nice round circles.

Next he added
blueberries.

He waited just a minute to let the pancakes cook.

Then he flipped them over.

And last, he added syrup.

The line for pancakes was enormous. But with four hands, George made quite a chef—and no one's plate was empty for long.

"I've been coming to this breakfast for years," a man said. "But I've never seen pancakes made like this before!"

"I've never eaten this many pancakes before," said a girl.

"I didn't even like pancakes before!" said another girl. And they all lined up for more.

When the man returned with his new assistant, he was shocked to see a monkey making pancakes. "This is no place for a monkey!" he yelled, and he began to chase George.

George hadn't meant to cause trouble. He'd only wanted to help. Now he only wanted to get away. Quickly, George found a place to hide, and the man and his assistant ran right by.

But where did George go?

When it was safe to come out, George jumped down. He was covered in syrup like a pancake — and he was sticking to everything! George was curious: could these napkins help him get clean?

No! The napkins only made it worse.

What George needed was some water to wash with...why, here was the perfect thing.

George climbed up.

This would do the trick for a sticky monkey!

George sat on the bench and splashed himself with water. But all of a sudden...

Splash! George was IN the water. What a surprise! George climbed up again and splashed back down. He'd never been in a dunk tank before, and he'd never had so much fun getting clean! Soon everyone

was having fun, and the line at the dunk tank grew even longer than the line for pancakes. Later, the mayor came by. "I've heard all about your delicious pancakes," he said. "You've made our fundraiser a big success and I have a special favor to ask you..."

At the end of the day, George got to present the money from the fundraiser to the president of the hospital. "Thanks to you, George, this has been our best year ever!" she said. "Will you come back and make pancakes again next year?"

George nodded and everyone cheered.

MARGRET & H.A.REY'S
Curious George
Feeds the Animals

Illustrated in the style of H. A. Rey by Vipah Interactive

Houghton Mifflin Company   Boston

This is George.

George was a good little monkey and always very curious.

One day George went to the zoo with his friend, the man with the yellow hat. A new rain forest exhibit was opening and they wanted to be the first ones inside.

But when they got to the new exhibit, the doors were closed. "We'll have to come back later, George," the man said. "Why don't we visit the other animals while we wait?"

First they stopped to watch a zookeeper feed the seals. When he tossed little fish in the air, the seals jumped up to catch them. Then they barked for more.

It looked like fun to feed the animals!

FEEDING
TIMES
10:00 AM
1:00 PM

"Would you like something to eat, too, George?" asked the man with the yellow hat, and he bought a snack for them to share.

When they stopped to see the crocodile, George remembered how the zookeeper had fed fish to the seals. He was curious. Would the crocodile like something to eat?

George tossed him a treat—and the crocodile snapped it out of the air!

Next they visited the koalas. George thought the koalas were cute. Here was a friendly one — she was curious, too. She wanted to see what George was eating, so he held out his hand to share.

George shared his treats with an elephant

and a baby kangaroo.

George was making lots
of new friends at the zoo. The
lion was already eating, but the
hippopotamus tried a snack.
Next he gave a treat to an ostrich.

Then George saw the giraffes.
What fun to feed a giraffe!
Giraffes usually have their
heads up high in the trees, but
George could see these giraffes
would be easy to feed.

But as soon as he held out his hand, a zookeeper came running.
The zookeeper looked angry. Was he angry with George? George didn't
know—and he didn't want to stay to find out. He slipped away...

and the giraffes were happy to help!

But where did George go?

He was trying his best to hide. But little monkeys can't stay still for long. When George wiggled, the zookeeper was waiting. "I see you!" he said.

Just then another zookeeper hurried by. "Come quick!" she yelled. "Someone saw the parrot!"

The first zookeeper led George to a bench.

"The parrot from our new exhibit escaped and I must help find it," he explained.

He told George to wait for him there, and before he left he said, "Don't you know you're not supposed to feed the animals? The wrong food might make them sick."

George felt awful.

He didn't know he wasn't supposed to feed the animals. He didn't want to make them sick.

George was looking at the treat in his hand when all of a sudden,

a big bird swooped
down and snatched it right up!
Now George knew he wasn't supposed to
feed the animals…but this one had helped itself.

A zookeeper passing by was happy to see George. "You found the parrot!" she said. "We've been looking for this bird all day."

When she saw George's snack, she said, "This isn't the best thing to feed a parrot, but a little won't hurt. Would you like to help me put him back where he belongs?"

George was glad to help after all the trouble he had caused, and together they went back to the exhibit.

"There's our problem," the zookeeper said, pointing to a hole in the netting. As the zookeepers discussed how to fix it, George had an idea. . . .

He climbed up like only a monkey can, and when he reached the hole — he tied the netting back together!

Meanwhile, the first zookeeper returned. "Catch that naughty monkey!" he yelled. "He was feeding the animals!"

"But that little monkey found the parrot," another zookeeper told him. "And look — he fixed the netting. Now we can open the exhibit."

When George came down, all the zookeepers cheered.

Finally the celebration began and the doors were opened. The man with the yellow hat was there, and he and George got to be the first ones inside!

As George walked in, the zookeepers thanked him for all his help. "Please visit anytime!" they said.

George couldn't wait to come back and see his friends. But next time he'd remember, unless you're a zookeeper...

MARGRET & H.A. REY'S
Curious George
Goes to a Movie

Illustrated in the style of H. A. Rey by Vipah Interactive

Houghton Mifflin Company   Boston

This is George.

George was a good little monkey and always very curious.

One afternoon George took a trip into town with his friend, the man with the yellow hat.

"Look, George," the man said as they walked by the theater. "The movie we've been waiting to see is here. If we hurry, we can make the next show."

"Two tickets, please," said the man with the yellow hat.

As they walked through the lobby, the smell of popcorn made George hungry. But when he stopped in front of the concession stand, his friend said, "Let's find our seats first, George. The movie is about to begin."

Inside the theater, they found two seats right in front. The man with the yellow hat whispered, "George, I'll go get some popcorn now. Stay here and watch the movie and please stay out of trouble."

George promised to be good.

George was enjoying the
movie when all of a sudden
a big dinosaur jumped onto
the screen. It made George
jump right out of his seat!

George was curious. Was he the
only one to jump out of his seat?
He looked around.

He was.

Looking around,
George saw a bright
light coming from a little
window at the back of the
theater. Was that what made
the movie appear on the screen?

Though he had promised to be good, little monkeys sometimes forget...

and soon George was at the back of the theater. But the window was so high, not even a monkey could climb up to see through it.

Usually there is a room behind a window, thought George. But how could he get inside?

Then he saw a door.

George raced up the stairs and peeked inside.

He saw a strange machine with two spinning wheels.

It was making a funny noise — and it was making the light that came through the window! Now he could see how the movie worked. But when he stepped into the room,

George was surprised to see a boy sitting in a chair. The boy was surprised to see a monkey standing in his room. In fact, the boy was so surprised, he jumped right out of his seat — and knocked the wheels right off the machine!

Downstairs in the theater, the audience began to shout and stomp their feet. They wanted to watch the movie...

but the movie was all over George!

George felt awful. The movie
had stopped and it
was all his fault.

"This is no place for a monkey," the boy said, working quickly to
unwind George and rewind the movie. "Why don't you wait by that
window while I fix this mess."

As George waited, he
looked out the window at the
audience and the big blank screen.
When he moved in front of the light that was coming
from the machine, he saw his shadow down below.
    This reminded George of a trick!

He arranged his hands just so . . .

and a bunny appeared on the screen.

Then George made
a dog.

And a
duck.

And another
dog.

"It's a puppy!" someone from the audience shouted.

Others joined in. "It's a bird!" they said. George made the bird fly away.

Then the audience saw George's shadow up on the screen. They were delighted.

"It's a monkey!" a child yelled, and the audience laughed and clapped.

"This is better than a movie!" said a girl to her friend.

Just as George was about to run out of tricks, the boy announced that the movie was ready to go. The audience cheered—once for the movie and once for George!

The audience was still cheering when the man with the yellow hat ran into the room. "I thought I'd find you here, George," he said, and he apologized to the boy for the trouble George caused.

"He did give me a scare," the boy said. "But thanks to his hand

shadows, everyone waited patiently for the movie to be fixed."

Then the boy restarted the movie. "Would you like a treat for your performance, George?" he asked.

And before the dinosaur appeared again on the screen . . .

George and the man with the yellow hat were back in their seats.

This time, with popcorn.

MARGRET & H.A. REY'S

Curious George

and the Hot Air Balloon

Illustrated in the style of H. A. Rey by Vipah Interactive

Houghton Mifflin Company   Boston

This is George.

George was a good little monkey and always very curious.

He was on a trip with his friend, the man with the yellow hat. It was the end of their vacation, and they wanted to make just two more stops.

They were in South Dakota so, of course, they went to see Mount Rushmore. George had never seen anything like it. "These are the

faces of four great presidents," a tour guide said. "George Washington, Thomas Jefferson, Theodore Roosevelt, and Abraham Lincoln."

"Look!" said a girl.
"There's something crawling
on George Washington's head."
The tour guide explained that some
workers were making repairs to the faces.
George watched the workers.

Then he saw a helicopter fly by. It was taking tourists for a close-up look. George thought that would be fun.

"Maybe we can take a ride later," the man said. "But now we need to leave or we'll be late for the hot air balloon race."

So they got back into their little blue car and before long they came

to a whole field full of hot air balloons. George was delighted to see such big balloons. He liked their spots and stripes and stars, but his favorite had a picture of a bunny on it.

RACE TODAY!

One balloon was not yet up in the air. Its owner was hurrying to fill it as a newspaper reporter took pictures.

The man with the yellow hat watched the balloon on the ground, but George watched the balloons in the sky.

He was curious: why didn't they fly away?
Then he saw the ropes.

A rope is a good thing to keep a balloon
from flying away, thought George. A rope is
a good thing to climb. . . .

Sometimes when a monkey
sees something to climb, he can't
help himself. He has to climb it.
George thought he would
climb just one rope then quickly
climb down.

But when George climbed
up, there was no way to climb
back down. The rope had come
undone — and there was only
one place to go.

UP

UP

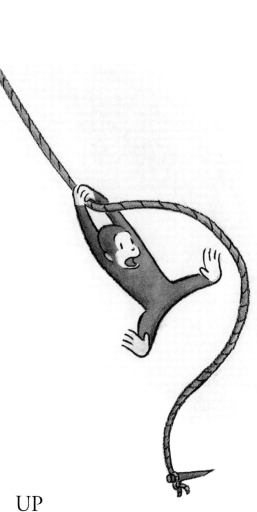

UP

went the balloon.
And George went
with it.

George flew higher and higher, and the people below grew smaller and smaller.

The man with the yellow hat was tiny. The newspaper reporter was, too. And the owner of the balloon wasn't very big...

but he was big enough for George to see that he was angry!

George felt bad. He didn't mean to take the balloon — he didn't even know how to fly it. As the wind whisked him away, he wished he had someone to help him.

But he was all alone.

George climbed into the basket. When he looked around, he found he wasn't alone after all. The race was on — and he was in the lead!

Together the balloons flew across the field and over the forest.
Now George was having fun. But before he knew it...

George was alone again, and all the fun was gone.

Flying by himself high in the sky, George was frightened. How would he ever get down? he wondered. Oh, if only he hadn't climbed that rope...

Suddenly the wind changed, and George saw something familiar.

He was excited—someone was sure to help him now. In fact, there was someone right in front of him!

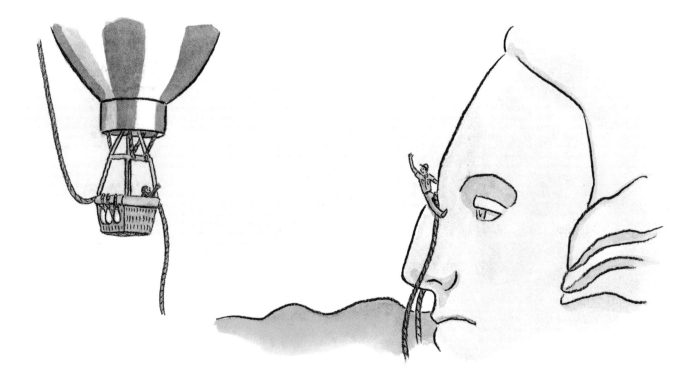

It was one of the workers — and he was stranded on George Washington's nose! George was so happy to see the worker he didn't notice how happy the worker was to see him.

Slowly, the balloon floated closer.

Would it come close enough? It did! The worker grabbed onto the rope and climbed up. Soon he was in the basket with George.

Hurrah, George was rescued!

Hurrah, the worker was rescued, too!

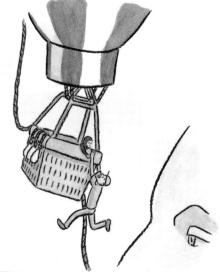

They sailed up over George Washington's head and landed safely in
a tree. Soon a whole crowd came to rescue them both.

The man with the yellow hat was happy to see George. The reporter was glad to have such an exciting story to report. And the owner of the balloon wasn't angry anymore.

Everyone had seen the rescue — George was a hero!

After the workers thanked him, George got a special treat — he got to ride in the helicopter.

The helicopter flew George and the man with the yellow hat once more past the presidents, then back to the little blue car.

As they drove away, the man said, "That was some vacation, George!"
George agreed. It was an exciting vacation. But they were both very
glad to go home.

MARGRET & H.A.REY'S
Curious George
in the Snow

Illustrated in the style of H. A. Rey by Vipah Interactive

Houghton Mifflin Company   Boston

This is George.

George was a good little monkey and always very curious.

One cold day George went to a winter sports competition with his
friend, the man with the yellow hat. They were outside all morning
and wanted to warm up with a hot drink.

At the ski lodge on top of the mountain, the man said, "George, why don't you wait at this table while I get some hot chocolate? I'll be right back, so don't get into any trouble."

George liked being on top of the mountain; there was so much to see! Why, there was something interesting.

George thought it looked like a spaceship.

He was curious. What was a spaceship doing on a mountain?

George forgot all about waiting for the hot chocolate...

and climbed in. A man in a racing suit saw him and said, "What are you doing in my sled?" He tried to stop George, but it was too late. The sled shot down the mountain—with George inside!

This is no spaceship, thought George. This is a rocket!

"Stop that monkey!" the
man yelled.

But George could not stop.
And there was no one to stop
him as he sped faster and faster
through the snow.

Suddenly the sled slipped
sideways — George didn't know
how to steer.

The sled swished through some trees

and whacked into a pole!

Luckily, George was not hurt, but this was not where he was supposed to be. Now how would he get up the mountain? George looked at the sled. It was stuck by the pole. He looked up the pole.

Now he could see how a little monkey could get to the top of a mountain. George climbed the pole, and

when an empty seat came close enough, he jumped!

What a view! From up in the air, George could see everything. As he rode up the mountain, he watched tiny skiers race down.

When he reached the top, George was happy to see the ski lodge.

This was where he was supposed to be!

George found the table. But he couldn't find the man with the yellow hat.

Where could he be?

George looked down the mountain.

There was someone who looked like his friend! Maybe his friend was going down to get George. But how could George get down the mountain this time?

If only he had another sled . . .

Why, here was a
monkey-sized sled.

George took the sled down

and gave himself a push. The sled
was quick to pick up speed on the
steep mountain.

George zigged this way and that way, then another way altogether.

He flew over a hill

and landed on the raceway!
"It's a monkey!" yelled a boy, and the crowd cheered.

"Look out, little monkey!"
someone yelled from the crowd.
   But George was going so fast
that the wind roared in his ears,
and he could not hear!

But George could see.
   He saw a skier right in
front of him.
   Could he stop?

No!

The crowd gasped as George crashed into the skier and flew up in the air. The skier went tumbling and his ski snapped right in half. When George came down...

he landed on the broken ski . . . and kept going!

The crowd was amazed. "What is he doing?" they asked. "Is he skiing? Is he sledding?"

"He's surfing in the snow!" said a boy.

George sailed down the mountain and came to a smooth stop.

What a show! The crowd cheered as George took a bow. No one had seen skiing like this before! When the skier arrived, everyone was glad to see that he was not hurt, and they cheered for him, too. Soon the man with the yellow hat arrived. He was glad to find George.

George was glad to finally find his friend. The man with the yellow hat made his way through the noisy crowd to apologize to the skier. "I'm sorry George caused so much trouble," he said.

"That's okay," said the skier. "I still have another race — and another pair of skis." Then he said, "That was some skiing, George!"

Later that day, the skier raced again—and won! It was a new record! The crowd went wild. They were still cheering when the skier found George at the finish line. "Thanks to you, George, this big crowd stayed to cheer me on," he said. "I couldn't have won without them—or you."

He lifted George to his shoulders and the crowd cheered once more for their favorite monkey skier, George.

The end.

MARGRET & H.A.REY'S

Curious George's Dream

Illustrated in the style of H. A. Rey by Vipah Interactive

Houghton Mifflin Company   Boston

This is George.

George was a good little monkey and always very curious.

After a long day at the amusement park with his friend, the man with the yellow hat, George was tired and glad to be home.

Soon dinner was ready.
But when George sat down
to eat, he was too small to
reach his plate.

"I'm sorry, George," the
man said. "I forgot to fix
your chair."

He put a large book on
George's chair and George
climbed up.

As he sat on the book that was set on his chair, George thought about his day. All day long he had been too small . . .

"Your hands are too little
to hold these baby bunnies,"
the manager of the petting
zoo told him.

"I'm sorry," said the
man operating the carousel.
"I cannot let you on. You
need a grownup to ride
with you."

"Maybe next
year," said the man
taking tickets at the
roller coaster.

175

But after a good meal and a good
dessert, George began to feel better.
When the dishes were finished,
the man said, "George, I have
a surprise for you," and they
went into the living room.

The surprise was a movie.
George was glad to watch a
movie — that was some-
thing he was not too
small to do!

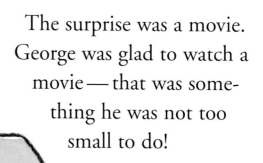

George was enjoying the movie, but it had been a full day and now he had a full stomach. Soon he could not keep his eyes open. The next thing George knew,

he was back at the petting zoo!
But this time something was
different: the petting zoo was
very small. In fact, everything
was small.

George looked around.
Then he looked at himself.
Maybe everything wasn't so
small after all, he thought.
Maybe he was...

BIG!

Uh-oh! This is not right, thought George. Then he remembered
the bunnies. Why, he was not too small to hold a bunny now. He was
not too small to do anything! What fun! George thought, and he went

to the bunny hutch. Now George could hold LOTS of bunnies, and he cuddled them to his face.

The bunnies liked George...

but the manager of the petting zoo did not. "Put those bunnies down," she said. "You'll scare them. You are too big!"

George didn't want to scare the bunnies. He put them down and turned to go.

Then George saw the roller coaster.
He was curious.
Was he big enough to ride it now?

Of course he
was big enough! If
only he could find a
seat big enough for him . . .

But the man taking tickets made George leave. "You cannot ride
this ride," he said. "You are too big!"

George was sad he could not ride, but he did as he was told.

"Catch that monkey!" someone yelled as George was leaving the roller coaster. "He's dangerous!"

People in the park became frightened. They began to run. They ran in all directions; but mostly, they ran AWAY from George.

George felt awful. He didn't want to frighten anyone.

He just wanted to hide. But where could he go? He was too big
to fit anywhere. Then George saw the carousel. He wouldn't need a
grownup to get on with him this time.

But this time George wished he had a grownup with him . . .

he wished his friend were here.

George sat on the carousel feeling lonely. Suddenly, someone called his name. "George? George?" It sounded like the man with the yellow hat! Could his friend be here to take him home?

George heard his name again.

It was his friend!

George wanted to jump into his friend's arms, but the man with the yellow hat was too small. How could he ever take George home now? The man called his name again...

"George," he said. "Wake up. It's time for bed. You fell asleep watching the movie."

George looked at his friend. Why, he wasn't small after all.

George looked at himself. He was not big!

Now George could jump into his friend's arms—and that is what he did.

As the man with the yellow hat tucked him in, George was happy to be in his little bed. It was not very big, he thought. But he fit in it perfectly.

George was just the right size.

Margret and H. A. Rey

Among children, Margret and H. A. Rey were best known as the parents of Curious George, the hero of their most famous books. "I thought you were monkeys, too," said a little boy who had been eager to meet them, disappointment written all over his face.

Not all of the Reys' children's books are about George, but they are all about animals. The Reys both loved animals, and one of the first things they would do when they came to a new town was visit the zoo. In Hamburg, Germany, where both were born, H.A. lived close to the famous Hagenbeck Zoo and, as a child, spent much of his free time there. That's where he learned to imitate animal voices. He was proudest of his lion roar, and once he roared for 3,000 children in the Atlanta Civic Auditorium, thus making the headlines in the *Atlanta Constitution* for the first and last time.

Over the years the Reys owned an assortment of animals: monkeys in Brazil, which unfortunately died on a trip to Europe; alligators, chameleons, and newts in New Hampshire; and dogs. They always had a cocker spaniel, and H.A. generally managed to get him into one picture in each of their books.

H.A. also wrote and illustrated two books for adults on astronomy. The books were, in a way, a by-product of the First World War. H.A., as an eighteen-year-old soldier in the German army, carried in his knapsack a pocket book on astronomy, the stars being a handy subject to study in those blacked-out nights. But the book was not much help for the beginning stargazer, and the way the constellations were presented stumped him. So, many years later, still dissatisfied with existing books on the subject, he worked out a new way to show the constellations and ended up doing his own books on astronomy.

H.A. started drawing in 1900, when he was two years old, mostly horses. At that time, one could still see horses all over Hamburg. He went to what in Europe was then called a humanistic gymnasium, a school that teaches Latin in the fourth grade, then Greek, then French, and then English. From this early exposure to five languages, H.A. developed a lasting interest in linguistics. He spoke four languages fluently and had a smattering of half a dozen others.

After school and the First World War, H.A. studied whatever aroused his curiosity—philosophy, medicine, languages—but he never attended art school. To pay the grocery bills while studying, he designed posters for a circus, then drew them directly on stone to make lithographs, an experience that came in handy in later years when he had to do the color separations for his book illustrations.

Margret received a more formal art education. She studied at the Bauhaus in Dessau, the Academy of Art in Düsseldorf, and an art school in Berlin. She even had a one-person show of her watercolors in Berlin in the early 1920s. Then she switched to writing, did newspaper work for a little while, and later became a copywriter in an advertising agency. At one point she wrote jingles in praise of margarine, an experience that left her with an undying hate for commercials. Always restless, Margret switched again to photography, working in a photographic studio in London for a short time, then opening her own studio in Hamburg just when Hitler came into power.

H.A. decided to leave Germany in 1923, when the country's postwar inflation had become so catastrophic that the money he received for a poster one day would not be enough to buy lunch a week later. He went to Rio de Janeiro, Brazil, and became a business executive in a relative's firm. Among other things, he sold bathtubs up and down the Amazon River. He pursued this rather uncongenial activity until 1935, when Margret showed up in Rio, too.

They had met in Hamburg just before H.A. went to Brazil. As H.A. told the story, he met Margret in her father's house at a party for her older sister, and his first glimpse of her was when she came sliding down the banister.

With Hitler in power, Margret had decided to leave Germany and work as a photographer in Brazil. The first thing she did when she saw H.A. again was to persuade him to leave the business firm. He did, and they started working together as a sort of two-person advertising agency, doing a little of everything: wedding photos, posters, newspaper articles (which Margret wrote and H.A. illustrated), and whole advertising campaigns. Four months later they married. The Reys went to Europe on their honeymoon, roamed about a bit, and finally went to Paris, where they planned to stay for two weeks. They stayed for four years, in the same hotel in Montmartre where they first took lodging. They might have stayed permanently had the Second World War not started.

In Paris the Reys created their first children's book. It came about by accident. When H.A. did a few humorous drawings of a giraffe for a Paris periodical, an editor at the

French publishing house Gallimard saw them and called the Reys to ask whether they could make a children's book out of them. They did—*Cecily G. and the Nine Monkeys*. After that they wrote mostly children's books, and it agreed with them. H.A. was always surprised to get paid for what he liked to do best.

In June 1940, on a rainy morning before dawn, only a few hours before the Nazis entered the city, the Reys left Paris on bicycles, with nothing but warm coats and their manuscripts tied to the baggage racks, and started pedaling south. They finally made it to Lisbon by train, having sold their bicycles to customs officials at the French-Spanish border. After a brief interlude in Rio de Janeiro, their migrations came to an end when they saw the Statue of Liberty as they landed in America.

The Reys took a small apartment in Greenwich Village, rolled up their sleeves, and were ready to start from scratch. Before the week was over, they had found a home for *Curious George* at Houghton Mifflin.

H.A. illustrated and Margret wrote, turning her husband's pictures into stories. Margret sometimes wrote her own books, such as *Pretzel* and *Spotty,* and H.A. did the illustrations, at times changing the story a little to fit his pictures. Doing a book was hard work for them and frequently took more than a year. They wrote and rewrote; drew and redrew; fought over the plot, the beginning, the ending, the illustrations.

Ideas came from a variety of sources: an inspiration while soaking in a hot bathtub; a news item in the paper; a piece of conversation at a party. Once they heard a biochemist tell how, as a boy, he had made a bargain with his mother to give the kitchen floor a thorough scrubbing in order to get money for a chemistry set. So one day, while his parents were out, he sprinkled the contents of a large package of soap flakes on the floor, pulled the garden hose through the window, and turned the water on. In *Curious George Gets a Medal,* George emulates this experiment with spectacular results.

The Reys' books were eventually translated into more than a dozen languages, and Margret loved leafing through copies of these foreign editions. It did not matter that she couldn't read some of the languages, such as Finnish and Japanese—she happened to know the story.

Based on Margret Rey's August 1994 essay for
THE COMPLETE ADVENTURES OF CURIOUS GEORGE

THE END!